DICK CHENEY

IN SHORTS

CHARLES

HOLDEFER

Sagging Shorts

ISBN: 978-1-944697-21-1 (paperback)

ISBN: 978-1-944697-22-8 (ebook)

Library of Congress Control Number: 2016954233

Sagging Meniscus Press

web: http://www.saggingmeniscus.com/

email: info@saggingmeniscus.com

These stories first appeared, sometimes in different form, in the following magazines:

"The Leo Interview" in *North American Review*
"My Inheritance, My Heritage" in *Nano*
"The Plans" in *Gargoyle*
"The Miüsov Festival" in *The Florida Review*
"Information Age" in *Los Angeles Review*
"Goodness Like a Fetter" (as "The Happiness Machine") in *Caliban*
"Bald Romeo," "Dick on a Plank" and "Community" in *Caliban Online*
"A Career in Public Service" (as "Professional Experience") in *FortyOunceBachelors*
"Full-Experience Christmas Greetings" in *Glib*
"A History of the Fruitcake" in *100 Words*
"At the Luxury Pet Shoppe" in *Crack the Spine*
"Why I Wear a Hat" in *Southern Humanities Review*

DICK

CHENEY

IN

SHORTS

"If I had a yaller dog that didn't know no more than a person's conscience does I would pison him."

The Adventures of Huckleberry Finn

CONTENTS

Prologue

Early Years

Achievement

Legacy

Book Club Questions · 133

Prologue

MY INHERITANCE, MY HERITAGE

"Hey! Come here."

He invited me into the bathroom, where he reached high in the medicine cabinet and pulled down an old tube of toothpaste. It was rolled up from the end, bunched and compacted, and resembled a snail. He unscrewed the cap and handed me the gnarled tube. "Squeeze some out," he said.

I tried, pressing my thumbs, but nothing emerged. "There's not any left."

He frowned. "Sure there is. Come on, kid. Take some."

So I tried harder. I pressed and squeezed and worked the tube till my finger joints felt as if they would snap—but nothing came out.

He held out his hand, shaking his head as I returned the tube. "You can always get a little more if you try hard enough," he said. "It's a question of attitude." With his big thumbs, he began to massage the tube. He pushed. He kneaded. "I've used this one all my life. And my fa-

ther used it before me. His father, too. Some things—"
he paused and his face reddened as he bore down, and
suddenly, a miniscule aqua squib emerged—"are eter-
nal!"

With his fingertip he wiped off the squib, displayed
it in the air as if for a larger audience, and then slowly,
deliberately, brought the fruit of his efforts to the tip
of his tongue. It disappeared. "Someday," he said, "this
tube will be yours, too."

Traces of blue were visible on his teeth, as if he had
bitten off a piece of the sky.

Early Years

THE PLANS

Like many people, my friend Herb had his demons, but what set him apart was that he kept them in a pen in his back yard. One night after dinner when we'd finished dessert and everyone at the table leaned back and felt the meal settle, he invited us to come out and take a look.

"Oh, they're not interested," his wife Marjorie told him. She smiled at Nancy and me. "Are you sure you don't want some more apple crumble?"

We shook our heads.

"Stuffed," I protested.

"They might want to see them," said Herb. "Not that I'm insisting. I constructed the pen myself. It's my own design. What do you think?"

"Oh, we could..." said Nancy. She eyed me across the table. I knew that she wasn't keen on the idea because she started work early the next morning. We had a long drive ahead of us back to North Platte. But I was intrigued. "Sure, why not?" I told them.

So, with a scraping of chairs, we got up from the table. Dicky, a skinny boy with butterscotch hair, trotted in from the living room. He'd been excused from his supper long ago in order to listen to "The Shadow." Now he seemed excited. "You're going to see them? I'm coming too." He ran ahead and flung open the screen door.

Outside it was dusk, daylight was dwindling, and the only sound was a low *thruhum thruhum* of cicadas. The air felt cool and smelled of growing green. As we moved across their patio and onto the grass, stars were beginning to appear above trees and the lip of the horizon. Dicky reached the pen first, his fingers curling in the chainlink.

In this light you could still see them scrabble and dart across packed dirt. They were very quick. Approaching the pen, Nancy took my arm and giggled. She was nervous, I could tell. Suddenly, so was I—yet at the same time I wanted to press closer and get a better look.

"Crazy, eh?" said Dicky, and shook the wires, rattling as much as he could.

"I don't know what he sees in them," said Marjorie, folding her arms in front of her. "I would never keep mine that way."

Herb had fallen back from the rest of us and now approached with his hands in his pockets. On the way he noticed a baseball in the grass, and paused to kick it toward the hedge where no one would trip on it.

"Come on, Dad," Dicky urged, "show them. Go ahead!"

The boy stepped aside for his father. Herb cleared his throat, then bent forward and spoke in a low, steady voice. "This is where you end up," he murmured, and activity in the pen increased, there was more scuffling. "This is as far as you go. We're safe now, aren't we?"

The scuffling intensified, and there was something plaintive in Herb's question, a pleading note, unlike anything I'd heard over dinner. Maybe it was the way he said "*we*." Earlier this evening, "we" had referred to everyone at the table as we'd passed around plates of food and spoken of property prices and promotions for soil conservation agents. Herb and I worked in the same field and had roomed together in college. We went way back.

"This is a good place to raise a family," he and Marjorie had agreed. "Dicky likes it here, too. Did he show you his ant farm?" Now Herb spoke toward the wire, "Do you miss me? Do you?"

He was answered with a shriek. This startled me, and I reeled back. Nancy recoiled, too. In the pen they ran faster and faster till they were just gray flickers, and Herb's beseeching voice was drowned out by little screams rising into the night sky.

Dicky ran alongside the wires, his feet moving in a jerky dance. Marjorie shook her head and clapped her hands over her ears. She mouthed words but it was impossible to make out what she was saying: it was like speaking into a wind. I nodded and pretended to understand while Nancy pulled at my arm. She wanted to leave. I think we were both unnerved.

Now Herb moved away from the wire and the noise level went down instantly. He turned to us with a sad, twisted smile. "So. There we go."

"Well, Herb," I replied. "That sure is, uh—something!" I didn't know whether to comfort or congratulate him.

The fighting in the pen slackened and Herb called over his shoulder: "I'm leaving you now."

This stirred them up again—in fact, it seemed to provoke and madden them. Once more it was impossible to speak, such was the vociferation. Dicky dropped to his knees beside the pen, laughing, while on the other side of the wire they whirled and screamed. Dicky picked up a stick and began to poke it into the cage.

When Herb saw this, he swiftly stepped forward and grabbed the boy by the arm and jerked him to his feet, gave him a shake. He pulled him away toward the house. He scolded, "What's the big idea? That's not nice."

"I was only playing. It didn't hurt anything."

"Son, you shouldn't tease them," Herb said, patting

him on the shoulder. "You'll see. You'll have your own someday."

Nancy and Marjorie hurried across the patio. Suddenly, all was silent again, except for the *thruhum thruhum* of cicadas. Herb released Dicky, and then leaned in close to me, and said softly: "If you want, I can send you the plans."

QUALITY TIME

Behold, a certain disciple was there, named Timotheus...
Him would Paul have to go forth with him; and took and
circumcised him...

Acts 16: 1, 3

He couldn't block the sound. *Sctick, sctick, sctick.* Yesterday was the first time he'd heard the copper edge on silica stone. Paul surely knew that he was listening. Perhaps it was a test.

Last night, lying on his mat, he was awakened by the same sound. He kicked and gasped and opened his eyes in the darkness, his heart pounding.

But no.

The room was still. There was no sound. Wait—he detected a faint, shallow wheeze from the nearby mat where Paul lay.

His teacher slept.

Morning came.

Sctick, sctick, sctick. This time it wasn't a dream. Timothy looked up from his text, unable to concentrate.

He pictured Paul in the next room, his bald head shiny as if oiled by the sunlight streaming in the window. Bent over his task, immersed.

Should he be grateful? Only a week ago, they'd paused under a laurel tree and spoken of the journey before them. (Two more hours of light? Three?) They drank cool swallows of water and inspected the horizon. While resting, Paul shifted the subject to Zipporah, wife of Moses, daughter of Jethro, who had used only a sharp stone to circumcise her son.

"She did what she had to do. She was no fool."

A smile played upon his lips. It was almost teasing. A joke? Yes, Timothy knew the text, too. It could not be unwritten. It *was*.

13

But for Paul the law also foresaw a personal solicitude. He wanted to reassure Timothy. It would be easier in *his* hands.

Use a stone? Of course not! His teacher loved him, had always been good to him. There was every reason for trust. Their relationship with the law was of a greater beauty. When David had cut off the foreskins of two hundred Philistines, it was a different time, riven by vengeance.

Paul spoke of something else altogether. A new vision.

Sctick, sctick, sctick.

Timothy remembered his father, an uncircumcised Greek, taking him by the hand when he was a child and leading him into a sun-glinted river. His father's penis was a ropy, floppy thing, protruding from a pair of fleshy apricots. It seemed so different from the nubby digit between Timothy's legs that he pointed and peed through every day, cradling in his fingers. His penis was a mere caterpillar. But maybe it was only a matter of time. Timothy would grow like his father, too. One day he would be tall, his arms thick and strong, and hair would sprout on his face.

His father's grinning white teeth shone out of his beard.

"Come here," he said.

His father bent and grabbed Timothy under his arms. He lifted Timothy to eye level. Behind him was the sky with moving flecks of passing birds.

"Ready?" he asked.

"For what?"

His father rocked back, then forward, heaving him through the air.

Timothy yelped, and then he smacked the water and plunged, thrashing and wriggling. It was frightful to leave the earth and be immersed in something else, an unchosen element. Terrible! He rolled and kicked, but he couldn't escape. He clawed but couldn't grip. He hugged but everything slid away. Oh, it was hopeless!

Then big arms seized him and lifted him out into the air. He could hear his father laughing. Timothy sputtered and gasped.

"It's all right," his father said. "You're just fine."

A voice came from the next room.

"Timothy. Come here."

When he uncovered himself, Paul acted busy and did not look down.

"Come closer to the window."

Timothy obeyed and positioned himself in the light. Paul put a hand on Timothy's shoulder.

"Bring your foreskin forward. Son, I won't hurt you."

Numbly Timothy reached for his penis. He grasped but it was in retreat, as if he'd stepped into a cold sea. Paul waited. Timothy was aware of his left leg trembling and he shifted to put more weight on this leg, to stop the shaking. He pinched the end of his penis, squeezing the skin upward as much as he could. Now Paul looked down.

"Yes. That's good."

Paul blessed him and gave thanks, and at the same time he lowered his hand to Timothy's wrist, helping him maintain his grip. Then his other hand reached under the linen on the table and Timothy saw a flash of the two-edged knife.

"Take a breath. You don't have to be silent. It's all right."

Timothy obeyed. He inhaled deeply and waited. Now Paul pinched with him. Timothy stared at the globe of Paul's head, the discrete bumps there. The blade felt cold.

Then suddenly everything went hot. Liquid leaked between his fingers. He screamed and reeled back. Paul waved towards the open window.

"Keep pressing!" Paul encouraged. "Press!"

Now Timothy was lying on the floor, the ceiling shimmering and floating.

"It's finished," Paul said, his voice blurry, distant. "You're fine. It's all right. But you can't let up. *Press*."

In a grainy corner of vision Timothy saw a bird in the sun eating something off the ground. But how could he be outside? He was still in the room. Paul put an arm around his shoulder, encouraging, coaxing, praying. Then vision rushed outside again.

I am eaten by fowls, he thought. This is only the beginning.

Bald Romeo

I.

A lacerated, bald Romeo.
Jesus with a beer gut.

II.

Oh, why so chary,

                chary,

                        chary?

III.

My own dog cheated me at cards.
Junior lit the match at my feet.

Goodness like a Fetter

Richie was home now, recently out of jail for beating up a clown. Aggravated assault. And there was Grandpa Will and Grandpa Willy Jr., Lynne and the baby Liz, with the Yellow Dog. The room was heated by a woodstove, flames licking around a sooty grate. *"What about me?"* Richie said. *"You all just going to sit there?"* The iron door of the woodstove whined softly when Grandpa Willy Jr. swung it open to toss in another log; the fire cracked and spat. Grandpa Willy Jr. dropped the log and jerked back, but not fast enough: sparks hissed through the air and found his trousers and the backs of his blue-veined hands. He slapped the backs of his hands, wincing, and shook his trouser legs. He was a small man with red weathered cheeks, a high nasal voice:

"Crazy stuff, that willow wood!"

The Yellow Dog, whose muzzle rested on a polished wooden cube, opened big sleepy eyes. The cube was attached with a ribbon to the dog's neck.

"Isn't it warm enough in here already?" asked Lynne. "I'm all in a sweat."

She unbuttoned her blouse and offered a breast to the baby Liz, whose eyes squinched as she began to nurse.

"I did it for Pop," said Grandpa Willy Jr. "Pop is cold. I think he's getting sicker."

Lynne sighed, and Richie crossed his arms in annoyance. Was this his coming-home party? He'd expected them to be more welcoming. He'd pictured himself at the center of a jolly circle, with a glass of hot punch in his hand. Maybe a few balloons? Some music? Was that so much to ask?

Instead, he was treated to the sight of old Grandpa Will, who sat on the edge of the bed with a blanket over his shoulders. He had the same weathered cheeks of his son, but his were rimmed by a dirty yellow beard. A violent shiver ran through him, and he gathered the blanket tighter. When the shiver was over, he scratched his head, smacked his lips and said nothing.

"You can't go around beating people up," said Lynne. "It's that simple."

"The clown started it," said Richie.

"Shush," said Grandpa Willy Jr.

"The clown came up to me and told me I was a fool," said Richie. "Was I supposed to stand for that? It was raining and there was mud everywhere on the ground and mud on the backs of the elephants, too. They were so dusty that when the first drops hit their hides they made little clouds, little puffs. There was something lonesome about that. I mean somebody ought to take care to wash the elephants! Doesn't anybody care anymore? Then it started to pour. I had to get out of there, I left the elephants and stepped under the tent because of the rain, you see, just minding my own business, no different from other people. But then this clown comes up and starts with me. Says I didn't belong there. Says it wasn't my *place*. This clown, with his purple eyes and painted mouth, talking about *place*. I told him that I didn't mean any harm, I was just getting out of the rain. You could hear it drumming like crazy on the canvas. It was the kind of sound that creeps inside you. There's something so lonesome about this circus—and what does the clown do? He makes a scene. In front of all those people! It was like he could look into my brain and so he just *spits* into it. Everyone saw him do it. He wanted to fight. I mean, he might as well've come out and asked me. So I mixed up the colors on his face good."

"I'm cold," said Grandpa Will, shaking his blanket. "I'm cold."

"We know," said Richie. "We're working on it, OK?"

Baby Liz began to cry, her lips a mewling rosebud. The Yellow Dog rose on crooked legs and tottered sideways across the room, its head and shoulders drooping under the weight of the wooden cube. Lynne jiggled the baby up and down, and the Yellow Dog cocked its head and wagged its tail.

"What's that around Seymour's neck?" Richie asked.

No one answered his question. Grandpa Willy Jr. hoisted another log out of the woodbox and shuffled toward the stove.

"It's full!" said Richie. "For Christ's sake. You're not gonna make any difference."

Grandpa Willy Jr. swung open the door. With a grunt, he heaved the log inside. Sparks rained on the floor and he stamped around him in a jerky chicken dance, putting out the sparks and keeping his balance by grasping his suspenders. Then he tried to close the door. But the log protruded—the door wouldn't shut. He tried to force the door, pushing with both hands, a series of little grunts escaping him. But Grandpa Willy Jr. was too weak. Richie turned away from the sight of him.

"Why?" he moaned.

"Get in there!" Grandpa Willy Jr. stood up straight, lifted a foot, and kicked feebly at the end of the log. "*Now-you-get-in-there!*" Miraculously the log slid in, and Grandpa Willy Jr. did not fall down. He bent over and swung the stove-door shut, and then turned to them, panting. He rubbed his hands together.

"Heavy stuff," he said. "Hedge."

"Do you have to do *everything* he says?" Richie asked. "Why, why do you let him order you around?"

"Thank you," said Grandpa Will.

"Don't mention it, Pop," said Grandpa Willy Jr.

From his perch on the edge of the bed, Grandpa Will cleared his throat and began to sing:

Here I raise mine Ebenezer
Where my hopes shall always be.
Let thy goodness, like a fetter
Bind my wandering heart to Thee.

While he sang, Grandpa Willy Jr. loosened the ribbon around the Yellow Dog's neck. He removed the polished wooden cube.

"What *is* that?" asked Richie.

"So you really don't know?"

Richie shook his head.

The cube had a little crank on one side, like a pig's tail. Grandpa Willy Jr. gazed at it fondly. "This is a humdinger. You wanna try it? For all practical purposes, it's a happiness machine."

He handed the humdinger to Richie and then knelt to pat the Yellow Dog on the back, inquiring, "How's the spine, old friend?"

"Huh?" said Richie.

"Go ahead. Try it. Be my guest."

Grandpa Willy Jr. scratched the Yellow Dog behind the ears and its liquid brown eyes blinked with a slow, sensual languor. He gave the dog's back a long, sweeping caress and suddenly a tremendous pink tongue lolled out of its mouth. "Easy fella," said Grandpa Willy Jr.

"How's this thing work?" Richie asked, cradling the cube against his stomach. "It's heavy."

"It's simple. You just turn the crank, and you feel happy."

"Oh come on."

"Try it! You'll see what I mean."

Richie grasped the handle—then stopped. He looked around. "This is some kind of gag, right? Have I seen this one before?" But no one answered. His eyes returned to the cube, and slowly, he gave the handle a turn. It made a gentle whirring. He paused, and then gave the handle another turn. He began easily, but gradually turned it faster and faster, the whirring assuming a higher pitch. He glanced up once, and then he bore down, his arm became a blur, his cheeks puffed and the polished wooden cube started to whine. The sound filled the room like a siren. Until with a cry he let go of the handle and shook his head in agitation.

"I don't feel a damn thing!"

The whirring handle spun free, on its own going slower and slower until there was just a *tick-tick-tick*, and then it stopped. Grandpa Willy Jr. scowled.

"Gimme that! There's nothing wrong with it."

He stood up and took the cube and nestled it against his chest, the other hand taking the crank.

"Must be your attitude," he said. "How do you expect anything to work with your attitude? Who knows what's in that skull of yours?"

His forehead furrowed as he began to turn the crank. His face was tense with concentration. His arm went round and round. The whirring was not frantic but it was steady. And then, gradually, his mouth relaxed. A slow smile broke out across his face.

"Yes," he said. "Yes."

His smile broadened.

"Oh yes!"

"Stop it," said Richie.

"*Oh, now that's n-n-nice. Positively timeless. Boy oh boy!!*"

"It's the stupidest thing I've ever seen!" said Richie.

"I feel great," said Grandpa Willy Jr., tapping one foot, then the other. "Light as a feather."

"Knock it off!"

"Whoa! Hee hee!"

Richie charged at him, and in the scuffle that ensued, he wrested the humdinger from Grandpa Willy Jr.'s hands. Grandpa Willy Jr. tried to grab it back, but he was no match for Richie.

"Hey!" he protested.

"You're messing with me." Richie glowered. "You're always messing with me. I shouldn't even listen."

Lynne buttoned up her shirt, the baby Liz balanced on her lap, little arms flapping the air. "*Please*, both of you. You're being upsetting."

"I'm cold," said Grandpa Will.

Grandpa Willy Jr. shook his head sadly and returned to the Yellow Dog, kneeling once more to pet its back. The Yellow Dog trembled and Grandpa Willy Jr. lowered his voice to a murmur.

"I don't know what we can do for you anymore, Richie. Don't you sometimes wonder why you turned out the way you are? I mean so awful. There are things

I haven't told you. Things nobody knows." He hesitated, as if lost in thought. "Richie, when you were born you had a soft spot on your head like any other baby but the problem was, your skull didn't meld together. With you, it took *years* for the soft spot to go away. Doctor said he'd never seen anything like it. In the meantime your brain was exposed to everything. That's not safe. When you were a toddler, learning to walk, we were scared to death you'd fall down and puncture your head. That's the reason your mother always made you wear a cap."

"What's that?" asked Richie. "What the hell are you talking about?"

"We used to have dreams," said Grandpa Willy Jr., stroking the Yellow Dog faster and faster. "Dreams too awful to describe. So messy—"

"No," said Richie. "That's not true!"

"Oh yes!"

The Yellow Dog was slobbering, its head bobbing up and down, and from side to side.

"Leave him alone," said Lynne.

Grandpa Willy Jr. stopped petting and wagged a finger at Richie.

"But we looked out for you. You never did puncture your head, you can thank us for that. Though you might have bruised it a bit."

"*Stop it right now!*" said Lynne.

The cube thudded on the floor and Richie stumbled toward the baby. He reached out with thick fingers to touch her head. Liz gurgled and smiled toothlessly. Richie's eyes widened, he jerked his hand away. He staggered to the window where he inserted his hands under his armpits: he shuddered.

"It's true," he said. "Lord God Almighty."

Grandpa Willy Jr. sighed, retrieved the cube and turned it over in his hands wistfully. He went back to the Yellow Dog and reattached the ribbon.

"Honey," Lynne said, "it's nonsense, that's what it is, and meanness. He just gets some sort of kick, stirring people up."

"How do you know?" Richie asked, lifting his hands and pressing the top of his head. His eyes grew misty. "Maybe it goes back that far. I got this loneliness on the brain, and if only you could drain it like water—"

Tears rolled down his cheeks, collecting in the corners of his mouth. Grandpa Willy Jr. came over and rested a hand on Richie's shoulder. "Aw, buck up, big guy." Richie began to pull away but Grandpa Willy Jr. hung on, adding: "Son, maybe we ought to give that humdinger another try, what'd'ya say? I know you want it." Richie looked straight ahead, not answering, but not turning away, either. "Come on, now." Grandpa Willy Jr. squeezed Richie's shoulder. "Let's ask Seymour."

"Richie," Lynne said, "don't listen to him."

Grandpa Willy Jr. pulled a handkerchief out of his pocket and offered it to Richie. "Pay no attention to her. Why, she's never tried it herself. She always makes excuses."

"No, not excuses," she said. "I would if I could. But that thing won't work unless you believe it will."

Grandpa Willy Jr. sighed and made another trip to the woodbox. "There's no use for a wench like you." Richie glanced at the cube and then at the woodstove and when Grandpa Willy Jr. approached with another log in his arms, Richie pushed his shoulder.

"Forget it, you old clown!"

Grandpa Willy Jr. staggered and dropped the log, which bounced on the floor, barely missing his toe. He continued backward and fell against the wall. His hands gripped behind him for balance.

"Enough!" he cried. "Leave! You're not welcome here."

"Let it go!" Lynne said.

"I'm cold, I'm cold."

"You're all against me," said Richie. "But I'll show you, just you wait. I'm gonna make my mark."

"Woo woo," said the Yellow Dog.

"I'm cold," said Grandpa Will. "The problem is, this room is too big."

Achievement

A Career in Public Service

Get a job!

Tie knot in ostrich neck, then feed beak spicy mice.

Turnover! Turnover!

Survey the feathered orifice with horror and delight.

Repeat! Repeat! Repeat!

Pray that what you're doing makes sense to the excretia.

A Shock and Awe Triptych

I. Security Memo

<*classified*> NSA announced today that in a China that is rushing wildly towards its own idea of economic development, the people long suspected of being immune to the AIDS virus should be adopted by a bipartisan resolution in both the House and Senate, no longer an all-male body. This change on the horizon whose bottom, sources close to the First Lady acknowledge, threatens to drop out, promises to affect investors in Standard & Poor's 500 Index (despite a P/E of 16), former independent counsel, Max Kessil, whose consumption of red wine has formed an effective antidote against clogging his arteries by low-density lipoproteins, said.

Cynics contend that my sister's husband Clay took early retirement from the phone company where he's worked all his life last year. Therefore, it was almost a surprise and a relief to arrive at my house and find Syrian children being instructed in Baden-Powell tones.

Since a pouch will be hung around each sinner's neck, you can use it over and over again like a professional wrestler oiled and stripped or, if you prefer, like a beaver making a pond that turns into a fertile meadow. No one will be killed in a consultative document. You might cast a shadow but you can decide against it.

II. What Really Happened

Why not cherries? The boy deserved a treat. Her son hadn't complained about staying home all the time. *Little old man,* she called him, because now that his baby teeth had dropped out in front, his smile had a gummy, senescent aspect. His jug ears and solemn eyes only added to the effect. Lately they'd played a game with an invisible cupboard.

"Little old man," she said, "get me some patience."

He stepped to a bare spot on the wall and mimed opening a door. He reached in and extracted an imaginary jar, which he brought to her, his hand gripping empty space in front of his chest. With his other hand, he unscrewed the lid.

"How much do you want?"

"Oh, a big dose this time."

His sober expression, his lopsided grimace, tempted her to smile, but she held it in, in order to prolong the game.

"All right," he said. "Three."

She nodded and extended her palm while he began to pinch out her allotment. One—two—three times he reached into the imaginary jar. Then he looked up at her, hesitating. He pinched out a fourth.

From the balcony of their apartment they looked down onto a courtyard where a neighbor kept birds. Their cages lined a wall of concrete blocks, and all day long you heard their singing and chirping. Their neighbor had large hairy arms and a big voice, and when he spoke to his birds, his words came up to them, too. *"Dinnertime, my beauties! Tup Tup!"* Recently there had been trouble when her son had urinated from the balcony into the courtyard.

"He's pissing on my birds!" the neighbor shouted. "Are you people crazy?"

"We're sorry!" she called. "It won't happen again."

She obliged her son to go out to the balcony and call down an apology. When he came back inside, she demanded, "What's the matter with you? What were you thinking?"

"But I didn't piss on his birds!"

"Don't lie to me."

They went back and forth, and it emerged that he'd been careful to avoid hitting the birds. But he'd been seized by a curiosity to see what it would look like to urinate from such a height, and he'd acted on it. In fact, he'd done it several times. He liked the way it looked. Today was the first time that he'd been observed.

"That's what really happened. I didn't mean to make trouble."

"Little old man, that's stupid."

Still, although she didn't tell her son, she didn't blame him too much. It was boring to be cooped up in the apartment. Your mind invented unlikely diversions. And the neighbor in the courtyard had been rude to her in the past. Even now, he'd jumped to inexact conclusions, yelling and waving his arms. So what if he loved his birds?

Unbidden, her son approached the invisible cupboard and reached down the jar.

"How much do you want?"

She trusted him to behave on his own; she decided to venture out. "I won't be more than half an hour, OK? There might be a surprise for you. And stay away from the balcony!"

The market was five minutes' walk. When she arrived it was almost deserted, and she bought tomatoes and zucchini. This won't take long, she thought, noting the price of cherries. She wouldn't buy them at this stall. At the other end of the market there was a fruitseller with a better selection. His cherries were likely to be cheaper, too.

She slipped her purchases in her bag and picked out a short cut between the stalls. When she was a child she'd come here to play, darting among tables and crates and around imaginary obstacles. She'd made her own world, beyond the voices of adults. "A beautiful morning for beans!" a man called from behind his display. She smiled and kept walking.

Then the sky ripped: a tearing sound, as seams of air were parted. Her head jerked up, but it was already too late. There were just receding dots on the horizon. Now the ground shook and knocked her off balance. She fell to one knee and the strap slipped from her shoulder. She lurched forward, regaining her footing and started to run, her bag spilling, leaving a trail of tomatoes.

On the horizon, puffs of dust billowed up the hillside. The booming reached her seconds later. Those hits were already far away, in other parts of the city. She didn't have far to go. She sprinted, dodging other people hurrying in the opposite direction, shouting and seeing each other but not seeing each other, intent on their destination.

She turned her corner and all was cloud. She pressed her scarf over her mouth, running toward her building. But it was confusing. No, this was the wrong street. She coughed and started to run again, and then she stopped. Her neighbor walked a half-circle, arms in front of him, scratching his shoulders, wailing. Suddenly she recognized his courtyard. It was now a hill, a pile of broken shards.

She ran toward the rubble and he stupidly stepped in front of her, still wailing. She pushed him aside and stumbled onto the little hill, her throat bursting, and when she slipped she caught herself with her hands and began sweeping at the pieces, the sounds of her cries interrupted by her panting hiccups as she clawed toward what was not yet visible.

III. Homefront Checklist

Strike out the cliché

1. Fuck you broke.
2. Charity went on strike.
3. What's funny is not a joke.
4. We the people died.
5. Mission accomplished failed.
6. Freedom of speech lied.
7. Jesus came unnailed.
8. Crowded at the top.
9. Meaning killed for spin.
10. Words are a sop.
11. Unseen grief within.

A boneheap by subscription!

INFORMATION AGE

No one can reproach him for not noticing candlelight
and pasty faces, powdering hills and pigeon runs past
windows and down lightless stairwells, charred teeth in
the towncenter. But what could he do? While wonder-
ing, he regularly checked his messages.

FULL-EXPERIENCE
CHRISTMAS GREETINGS*

Helen didn't mean any harm when she took the Christmas card off the rack. She was shopping for something special to send her daughter Melissa who was doing her second tour of duty with the 1st Armored Division. She reached for a shining red and green card that had attracted her attention.

In reaction to her touch, it ejected a gust of pine needle fragrance. Electric *Season's Greetings!* pulsated in her face. For several seconds there was the tinkling melody of "Winter Wonderland" and then, quite distinctly, the gurgling of baby Jesus.

She opened the card, and a snowball rolled out.

"My goodness!" she exclaimed.

"You'll have to pay for that," the man at the counter said.

---

* $29.95. Sales tax and shipping not included.

COMMUNITY

So I downed my drink and hitched up my pants and moved out to the center of the dance floor. Everyone was there—not only Marty and Leonore and Condoleezza and Connie Sandmeier's ex-husband's girlfriend's little brother, but Mr. Barnley and Mrs. Botkins, my second grade teacher, and Sally (who was wearing tight shorts and looked fabulous) and Crazy Lyle, of course, with that damn parrot on his shoulder, but it was a different one, I think. Bigger and greener with a flesh-ripping beak. Anyway, it was my song.

And what can I say? I had the moves! That vibe to the nub of my spine! No partner for me, never mind—the flashing lights bounced off the inner hollows of my eyes. The floor moved beneath my feet. *Oooh, felt good*.

For a time—can't say how long—there was only the music. *Hooooooo*. Till, by degrees, I became aware of voices. Calling: "Go! Go! Go!"

Oh, now I really shook it! My song, and I gave it everything I had!

"Go! Go! Go!"

And then, a thought came over me. *What do they mean?*

Legacy

DICK ON A PLANK

(Washington) Former Vice-President Dick Cheney surprised observers by enthusiastically praising Hillary Clinton and confessing to an irresistible urge to "pinch her little cheek."

He also admitted that he lied about Iraqi weapons before the war, and that the Bush team failed at nation building.

Mr. Cheney made these statements over the weekend in a secret interview at an undisclosed site, where he was strapped to a plank with a sheet wrapped around his face, on which water was poured until he experienced a gag reflex.

He also announced that he was also pleased to confirm that U.S. interrogation tactics have respected human dignity and international law.

"Americans have never tortured," he said. "Why can't people get that straight?"

When pressed for details, he elaborated, "Listen, I don't always see eye-to-eye with journalists, but in interviews I've never experienced organ failure, or even the sensation of organ failure, OK? And I really appreciate the fact that you didn't bend my glasses."

In a lively conversation conducted while naked, Mr. Cheney revealed seldom-seen sides of himself. At times he seemed evasive or inclined to squirm. But several themes emerged again and again as the former Vice-President worked to stay on-message. He complained of being misunderstood, and a number of times he was heard to remark, "Why's it so cold in here? *Why?*"

Mr. Cheney also displayed a more tender and emotional side than is sometimes apparent in his public appearances. Asked if he was still optimistic about the future, he said, "*Ahhhhhhhhhhhhhhhhh!*" and "*Grruuuuuu-urrr!*"

Later in the same interview, Mr. Cheney confessed to firing shots from a grassy knoll, to smuggling explosives into the Maine, and to tipping off Roman soldiers at Gethsemane. He also admitted that he was responsible for the deaths of the dinosaurs.

THE WORLD'S OLDEST CATFISH

"No, it's not that kind of phantom penis, not like with my legs. It's different. I can see it, too."

As he spoke, a television on the wall played the theme song of a game show.

"See it?" the doctor asked. "What do you mean?"

His patient shifted his head on the pillow and faced the ceiling, a shape flickering across the tiles. He winced.

"It follows me around. Even when my eyes are closed."

From a nearby bed, an intubated man with no nose said, "It makes him very irritable."

They ignored him.

"You mean in your dreams? Is that when you see it?"

"Yeah, in dreams but also when I'm awake. It's disturbing. Actually, I think I see it *more* when I'm awake. It floats up. And if I close my eyes, it's still there. This penis." He cupped his hand, then let the hand drop.

The doctor lowered his voice. "Take your time."

"What do you want me to say? It hangs under my eyelids. It's got this little head. It's not like I recognized it immediately. First I thought it might talk and it took me a while to work out what kind of head it was, that it wouldn't speak to me. It's like something I inherited and didn't ask for, maybe even from the time before I got hurt, before I ended up here. But I don't want it, see? Actually I hate it and to tell the truth I *blame* it. But does that make any sense? Some little dick?"

The noseless intubated man said, "I don't got anything like that. Peniswise, I'm OK. But sometimes there's a mosquito flies around the ward and it bugs the hell out of me."

The doctor sighed and turned to him. "Please don't interrupt. Someone will get to you later, all right? I promise."

"Oh, of course you will," said the man without a nose with a tube in his trachea. "All of us here are heroes, right? Everybody cares about us. We're an example to children everywhere. That's the deal."

The doctor turned back to his patient. "Did you have any history of hallucinations prior to your arrival here? It could be your medications, but we need to know more, if we're going to get to the bottom of this."

"No. It's only recent."

Ding! Ding! Ding! went the television. There was a rush of applause from the studio audience.

"Doc, you say 'we,' but who is that?" called the intubated man who was lacking a nose. "I bet you had other priorities than military service. Am I right? Tell me if I'm right. Don't get me wrong, though. I don't mean it personal. But look at me!"

"*Please*," the patient pleaded, "could you move me to another bed? I've told him to be quiet but it doesn't work. How can I rest? The V.A. must have another bed."

The doctor nodded. "Sure, I'll look into that. Of course."

"You know I went to college, too!" said the man who was intubated, bereft of a nose. "I was in the drama club. *'If the cause be not good, the king himself hath a heavy reckoning to make, when all those legs and arms and heads, chopped off in battle, shall join together at the latter day and cry! It will be a black matter for the king that led them to it.'* I didn't get the part, but I know that shit. Barcelona!" he barked at the television.

The doctor reached for his patient's hand. "We'll get you moved. And remember, you're home now. One day, we'll get you out of this place. That's our mission."

"All the best parking places are just waiting for us," said the intubated noseless man. "They're reserved."

"Shut up the fuck up!" the patient shouted. "You hear me?"

The doctor stood. "Listen, we're not going to do it that way." He turned around. "And you—it's the least you can do to have some consideration. This is not a time for jokes."

"You got that right. Look at me." He was intubated and had no nose. "If you think this is some kind of frickin' joke, you've got another thing coming."

"That's not what I meant."

"I'm not gonna disappear. You follow? I'm not gonna be forgotten." He pointed to the television. "At least twenty, I'd say."

The caption asked: "*The age of the world's oldest catfish ???*"

The doctor looked up. "More like thirty."

"Fifty?" said his patient, then clapped his hands over his eyes and shuddered.

"The age of the world's oldest catfish is...sixty-seven!" said the beaming television host, and ran his hand over his hair.

THE MIÜSOV FESTIVAL

She would've forgotten that a new season started this evening if her husband Barry, a large man who practiced each Thursday night at his judo club letting his body strike the mat with tremendous smacks, hadn't said to her,

"Hey, don't you have one of your nasty movies tonight?"

Rita threw down her magazine. Why, yes, that was right! Her membership pass had arrived in the mail weeks ago. She jumped out of her chair and rummaged in a drawer among pizza coupons and individually wrapped butterscotch candies until she found the envelope from the Chilton Theater. She checked the date. Yes, indeed, the season began tonight, at 7:30, with the first of a series of films by P. Miüsov. She buttoned the side of her skirt, looking around for where she'd kicked her other shoe.

"Have fun," said Barry, giving her a kiss, and then, as he tromped out the door with his duffle bag over his shoulder, a low laugh escaped him.

Not even time to eat, she thought, swiftly gathering up her coat and purse. She caught the first bus downtown and arrived almost on the minute. There was no line; she felt once more the pleasant surge of anticipation as she showed her pass at the window, and a yellow and green striped ticket whished back to her. She knew nothing whatever of this Miüsov, but she'd always had good luck at this theater. She walked across the red carpet which was spotted with soda stains and let the usher tear her ticket, and then pushed through the swinging doors.

The Chilton was a small cinema, yet upon entering Rita always felt a sense of space, with the rows and rows of mostly empty seats, beneath a pearly screen which promised still more space, like a window. She proceeded down the aisle and took her favorite place at the center of the third row, not far from a bald man she recognized, who always sat at the end of the same row with his coat on and his collar up, partially obscuring his jaw. He flicked a glance at her beneath his glasses and then averted his eyes. They'd never exchanged a word. She opened her purse and turned off her cell phone, and then reached down and discreetly pulled off her shoes. She unbuttoned the front of her jacket, and crossed her legs. There.

Rita had certain expectations when it came to watching movies, conditions that must be met. Getting comfortable, obviously, was one of them but she also demanded to be spared all exterior noise and sensation. This was an article of faith that she wished everyone would observe, even with television; she preferred to watch with undivided attention and then talk afterward. But this wasn't possible with Barry. He was exactly the opposite: he loved to talk while a movie ran, to comment, to cajole, ask questions. He couldn't wait for commercials, and in public theaters was almost as bad. At regular intervals he spoke to the screen—as if it strangled him to be silent for more than fifteen minutes. Sometimes he even forgot to whisper, and people hissed at him in the dark. Rita couldn't bear this, and she would've throttled him, if it weren't for love. In fact it was fortunate that they had different tastes in movies, which made easy the current compromise: she let him speak as much as he liked when they watched television and his favorite DVDs at home, and he didn't ask to go along with her to the movie theater. It was a satisfactory solution. A marriage depended on such arrangements, she thought. The lights dimmed; the screen lit up.

A wrinkled face appeared, as creased as any Rita had ever seen, ancient, taking up the entire screen, blinking; a lone violin scratched plaintively. A title flashed across the face and disappeared, and a second later the subtitle translated, *Last Harvest*. The aged face smiled, with teeth the size of a child's, worn. Credits scrolled down the face in steady succession, names that were meaningless to Rita. Then she realized that the smile had become clenched, and tears were rolling down the cheeks. The eyes glowed. Burning eyes. Until the scene changed to a wobbling image of peasants in a field, bent over their work. The violin scratched on.

The film turned out to be a love story of a young woman with plump cheeks who, while she worked, smiled from time to time at a young bearded man in tall black boots. The young man looked back at her, very earnest, and stroked his wispy beard. The ancient wrinkled face, presumably the young woman's grandmother, watched them furtively and sometimes smiled, too, if she wasn't weeping as she gathered in the shocks. The movie was clearly very old, its black-and-white faded to a grainy grey, which made it hard to read the subtitles, because they blended in with the scenery. Much of the dialogue was lost. But Rita was able to follow the story, with its recurring incident in which the young woman gazed at the young man at night across the blazing fire, her round cheeks hinting at a flirtation, and he looked up, their eyes meeting for a moment, before she looked away. It seemed one of them might speak in the wavy light, but this never happened. The story showed them at work, and eating—there was much skinning of small animals, and roasting—and at the end of the film the grandmother lay down in the field, holding the young woman's hand, and gasped her last breath, while the young man turned his back and walked away as it began to snow. The violin scratched. He disappeared over a hill.

The lights came on, and the bald man at the end of the row coughed in approval. Rita put on her shoes, and stood up to button her jacket. She noticed that her knees hurt. They throbbed.

When she got home, Barry had already returned and was leaning over the aquarium, sprinkling fish food. His hair was wet from his shower.

"How was your depressing movie?" he asked.

"Don't say that," she told him. "You always say that about movies."

"No I don't. Depends on the movie. Movies you go to at that theater—hey, those are definitely El Depresso, the way they pretend to be so serious. What did you see?"

"*Last Harvest.* And it was very funny."

She noticed her jaw was sore; it actually hurt when she spoke. She wondered if she'd grimaced too hard during the film.

"A riot, I'm sure," he said. "You hungry, in those bones? I'll heat you up some chili."

"No." Only now she realized she hadn't eaten a thing all night—yet it was true, she wasn't hungry. She said, "Too much popcorn, you know."

He came up to her and put his hands on her hips. With a little push-pull, he turned her skirt completely around. "Look at you," he said. "Rita, you're gonna snap, you get much smaller. You got to take care of yourself."

Next Thursday night the film was *The Burnt Huts*. Instead of the lone violin there was a full orchestra which plucked and swelled as the peasants gathered together in a forest, carrying a coarse-shirted leader on their shoulders. He was a young man with dirty streaks on his face. He exhorted them, and they cried out toothlessly. They began sharpening birch sticks. Meanwhile, in a nearby church of stone and smoking candles, an aristocrat sipped from a goblet. He tied up his velvet breeches. They were velvet, Rita was sure, and probably scarlet, though in black-and-white she couldn't be certain, especially with this print, which didn't look black-and-white: the movie appeared to have been shot in brown. But at least it was easier to read the subtitles.

"My lord," said a priest with circles under his eyes, "the peasants are revolting." He uncorked another bottle.

The aristocrat ran his tongue around his lips. "I've always thought so." He held out his goblet.

Then the peasants had their say. At the signal of their leader, they stormed into the church, a swarming mass with pointed birch sticks in hand, breaking down doors and crashing through windows, upsetting candles and pews. In the climactic scene, after a flaming beam fell with a shower of sparks on the fleeing priest, the angry mob impaled the aristocrat at least one hundred times. At least one hundred, Rita was sure; she looked away twice, and both times she looked back, they were still at it, jabbing. How could there be that much of him left? she wondered. Clearly, Miüsov didn't hesitate to splice and repeat the same sequence, without shame. Over and over, the aristocrat's mouth fell open, cried out.

The next day at work Rita experienced pain each time she took a deep breath. A stab in her side. She worked at Essential Vinyl, a used record store, and was mainly responsible for online orders and bookkeeping for her boss Mitch, a wiry, fidgety man who was pretty, yet with lines on his face that he was proud of. His retired parents in Arizona financed the business. Mitch would stand behind the counter with an unlit cigarette in his mouth and his eyes half-closed, wiggling his fingers in front of his waist whenever a favorite guitar solo came over the store's sound system. The last few days he'd talked obliquely to Rita of edible underwear, made of a licorice product of high elasticity, which he said could be purchased for less than twenty dollars. Small sizes. Rita had expressed no interest in the subject. But this morning as she walked around the store with small steps, avoiding deep breaths, Mitch's lip curled up into a smile; he swayed to the music and asked, "Guess what?"

Rita looked up from the Siouxsie Sioux bin she was mechanically counting, one more time.

"What?"

"I'm wearing 'em."

Mitch swiveled his hips, and then he kissed the air.

Rita stared, trying to suppress what was rising in her throat, but she couldn't—she laughed, hard, but only for an instant, because pain shot through her chest; her laugh became a croak. It was a racking pain that made her bend over and catch herself against the counter. The blood ran out of her face and she stood before him, pale, her lower jaw trembling.

Mitch watched her, wide-eyed. "Whoa. You settle down now."

"I'm not well," she told him, in a tight voice.

Mitch became confused. "How's that? I—I make you sick?"

"No, no. I've been like this all morning."

"Oh. Why didn't you say so? You could've stayed in bed."

Rita thought: You wouldn't have paid me.

"Really," he went on, "there's no point in spreading your germs around here. You want to go home?"

"Yes, I'll go."

But she didn't go home, she went straight to the doctor. She described all her symptoms without mentioning the Miüsov Festival. What could I say? she asked herself. She searched her mind for an explanation. "It's just so much *soreness*," she told the doctor, who seemed puzzled, too. She gently touched Rita's chest, and when Rita uttered a cry of pain, she suggested an X-ray.

When the results arrived, the X-ray showed three cracked ribs.

"But how could it happen?" she exclaimed. "I haven't fallen, I haven't had any accidents."

The doctor was nonplussed.

"People have been known to crack them even laughing," she said.

So Rita tried to be careful, protect herself. Barry did his best to help her. At night she crawled onto him, feeling positively light-headed from an entire day of not breathing too deeply. She rubbed slowly against him, gripping his shoulders and, in a short time, she forgot about her pain and felt only her smooth pleasure, its rhythm. She breathed freely, on the verge of release.

Afterward, she wondered if perhaps she were healed. The best home remedy, she thought. But when she coughed to test herself, the pain flashed. The soreness was still there. Oh yes—there was no pretending.

She kept going to work at Essential Vinyl, but now that Mitch was warned of her ribs, she wasn't expected to talk much or laugh. This was a great relief.

"When you're better," he said, stroking his chin, "we should have some fun. You ever had a sex slave?"

"Maybe I'm not interested, Mitch," she said. "You know?"

He smiled and leaned over the cash register. His eyes quickly looked her up and down, then flitted away, nervous.

"Would you say that I'm a slut?"

Rita was going to walk away, but she paused to reply, "Listen, that's not what I meant."

His hips swiveled again, like the other day.

"But would you say it? Please?"

Now she turned.

"Hey, come on!" he called.

Rita shared with no one her doubts about the theater. But try as she might to find another explanation, she couldn't get round the fact that her soreness began immediately after the first Miüsov film, and had worsened considerably after the second. But these stories, what do they have to do with me? she thought. They're just strange old movies, and depressing, like Barry says. How could they affect me? Just a bunch of dead actors.

She did a name search on the Internet for Miüsov but none of the hits that concerned films by a person of that name were in English or in a language that she could understand. None of the movies she'd seen were available in DVD or other formats. She telephoned the theater, but the employee who answered could tell her very little, and at first was confused because there were several series running concurrently at the Chilton. "The Miüsov Festival!" Rita insisted. "Thursday nights!"

Eventually she talked to an assistant manager who read to her from the brochure she already had. There was a short entry describing each film, and about Miüsov it said:

> *These long overlooked masterpieces by Pyotr Miüsov have only recently been rediscovered and can now speak to another generation.*

There was a list of titles, and for next week, *The Three Heads*.

That Thursday Rita felt better. She could laugh again, though she didn't let on to Mitch. She could lift both arms above her head, and felt no pain unless she stretched to her utmost, grabbing air.

For dinner that night she and Barry put a chicken in the oven, and as always happened with their chickens, half of it melted into a yellow pool at the bottom of the pan. Then, before serving it, Barry soaked up the grease with slices of bread, salted and peppered them, and folded them into his mouth. He politely didn't do this at the table, respecting the fact that this custom disgusted her. He sneaked the slices while he prepared the salad. She watched his back, knowing what he was doing, and pondered the fact that he'd have a heaping bowl of ice cream for dessert, too. Someday, she told him, his body wouldn't be able to keep up. He'd have to change! If not, he could count on a serious problem. But as for now Barry was big without being flabby, an active, largeboned man, burning with a teenager's energy. Healthy as a tree. He would eat his impossible meal, and then jump up from the table and go practice judo. Bounce around. She saw the thick fingers which gripped his glass of iced tea, which he swilled, and felt a bemused fondness for him. Those big digits, his fistiness. He seemed an altogether different beast than she. More than once she'd taken one of those fingers and slipped it into her mouth, to taste him. Rita shifted in her chair; their dissimilarity stirred her.

After the meal, when he gathered up his duffle bag, she surprised herself by asking, "Can I come along?"

Barry was surprised, too. "Well, sure. It's not a demo tonight, though, just a practice session. Don't you got your movie?"

"Aw, movie," she said. "Maybe I'll try something else for a change."

So she sat on a folding metal chair on the periphery of the mats at the martial arts dojo while Barry and a dozen of his friends slapped and slammed and sweated on the mat. How they went at it! Barry had the second highest grade in his club, and no one sweated more than he did. How he could sweat! Rolling, rolling, rolling off him. As he'd warned her, it was only a practice session— not very interesting if you weren't a true fan. Twice a year Rita went to public demonstrations, which were much larger and took place in a vast auditorium. These bored her on a grander scale: 500 bodies smack-smack-smacking on the mat, endlessly. She attended out of loyalty in the same way he went to her family reunions.

Tonight her tailbone ached, but it wasn't one of her strange aches, it was just the folding chair. She shifted her bottom and wondered what she was doing here. Why, really, should she avoid a Miüsov film if she wanted to see it? Why? What was there about Miüsov films, anyway? What did she see in them?

She thought about how Barry and most people went to the movies in order to escape—at least that's what they said, and it must be true, for them, the old line about how movies offered a diverting alternative, a nourishing fantasy in which they could dream of being their heroes, sharing their qualities and adventures. These stories made the everyday world sweeter.

But such stories could only go so far, Rita thought. Their diversion had nothing whatever to do with why she was attracted to certain movies. In truth, there wasn't a single character in either of the Miüsov films that she could identify with, aspire to be, or fantasize about. She hadn't the slightest desire to enter those worlds! What's more, she couldn't help noticing the subterfuge behind what she was watching, the choppy camera, the caked make-up on the aristocrat's face that was vaguely humorous even as he cried out in agony.

Then why she felt attracted, she could not pin down. When Rita was younger, she didn't often go to these kinds of movies; she usually went to the latest release, with her latest guy. With time, though, she'd started asserting more choice for herself, and she'd become a regular at this theater. It had happened gradually, a sort of fascination reminiscent of the temptation that she had felt to take a deep breath after she had cracked her ribs, just to see if the pain were still there. Her eyes opened *wide* each time she winced. The other people she saw at the Chilton didn't seem like her, as far as she could tell. The older ones reminded her of her former high school teachers but red-eyed and gone to seed, college professors maybe; the younger ones looked like scenesters with money and ironic tattoos, the same types who slinked through Essential Vinyl. The bald man could've been anybody's retired uncle who'd come in off the street. Rita was alone here, completely alone— yet she returned again and again.

Even now, as the bodies slapped on the mat, bare feet arced through the air—she wished she were at the Chilton, and reproached herself for cowardice.

I can see any damn movie I feel like! she thought. No one's stopping me. The rest is just coincidence. Madness.

Still, in the car on the way home as Barry steered

with one thumb while sucking down a cold drink, she decided to ask a favor, to be sure.

"Say, BeeBee, next week, do you think you could skip the judo, and come along to the movies with me?"

He looked over at her, the straw in the corner of his mouth.

"O-Okay. If you say so."

She nodded, pressing her fingers into the back of his neck; for a moment the car veered.

"Will it be depressing?" he asked. "Will we punish ourselves?"

She took her hand away, frowning.

"Hey, come on. Just teasing," he said.

Barry had a gallon bucket of buttered popcorn on his lap when the lights went down. Tonight's feature was called *Coals.* There was no music at the beginning, just the credits flashing on a fire in a grate. This film must have been made later in Miüsov's career, for it was in color—though a tepid sort of color, like watching a film while wearing sunglasses. Yet that really was *orange* up there, and *red*.

The scene shifted to a circle of dancing devils. They pranced and sang, a capella, around a hapless-looking family.

"What the hell," said Barry. "What is this?"

Rita didn't answer. The song continued, the subtitles flashed:

> *Burning depths for you, my dearies,*
> *Burning depths for you!*

"What are they doing?" Barry asked.

"What does it look like?" Rita whispered. "They're dancing! They're singing!"

"Uh huh. Popcorn?"

The devils began to poke the people, making them cry out. Sometimes they poked them one at a time, eliciting a string of cries; other times they poked them all at once, prompting a chorus. When the people weren't crying out, they begged for mercy.

"What's happening now?" asked Barry.

"Just watch," she hissed. "You have eyes."

The story unfolded that the devils were awfully busy down in hell and worried that they might not be able to spend enough time with the family and give them the attentions that they deserved. There were heated arguments between two devils in particular about the problem. One maintained that they'd just have to settle for less, under the circumstances, while the other, a sickly devil with a clean-shaven, sensitive face, said No, they should not be denied—standards must be met! Barry quieted during this part, and seemed absorbed in their discussion; Rita recognized the same actors who were peasants and nobles in the previous film, who now wore Micky Mouse-type shorts, with attached pointed tails. These were sorry-looking tails, in truth; one firm yank and they would surely come off in your hand.

At one point, a young man of the condemned family made a break for it, tried to run away, but he didn't get far. Devils swarmed after him, and when they caught him, he was sheepish, trying to pretend that Oh no, he wasn't really trying to run away, not him. The devils laughed at these words and, horning him one after another, made him mighty sorry.

Rita began to be nervous. The laughter, the cries sounded almost the same.

The ending contained a surprise twist: tired and exasperated by the family, who did nothing but complain and make difficulties the whole time they were there, the devils settled their dispute by sending the family back to the world above, where others would have to put up with them.

The lights came on. The small audience began to file out. Rita noticed the bald man appeared stooped and weary as he exited the row. He didn't look back. She turned to Barry.

"That wasn't bad," he said, as she stood up gingerly. She noticed no soreness. Barry helped her with her coat, smiling. "No kidding," he said, "that was something. Who would think of all that?"

"Miüsov," she told him.

At the bus stop Barry talked with interest about the film. He said he was glad he'd come. "Is there another one next week? Maybe I should see it."

"No, the series lasts just a month. That's the end of the festival."

Somehow, she felt sad. "Oh, well," he said. Rita felt an emptiness inside, a horrible sense of being separate and incomplete, such as she'd rarely experienced. She felt she could cave in on herself. "Ah Sweet Bone," he said, kissing her on top of her head and then peering beyond her, down the street for the bus. "Maybe we shoulda drove," he said. She grabbed him by the belt.

"Barry, do you believe in hell?"

He looked down, grinning. "What? Hell? I don't know. Not a hell like that. If there is something out there I hope it's heaven. But it's pretty iffy either way, for my money."

She pulled away from him and thrust her hands in her pockets. She felt embarrassed, out of breath. He touched her hair. "Hey, what is it?" She didn't answer, didn't even look at him, and then the bus rolled up, the doors swished open. They climbed on. Barry kept his hand on the small of her back, though she hardly noticed it.

As she moved down the aisle she imagined what all these passengers would look like in devil suits. Then she stopped herself, profoundly annoyed at the image, its stupidity. Such nonsense! she thought. I don't believe it. First thing I'd do is pull off their tails!

But after they took their seats and the image was dispersed, she still longed for something else. She felt hopelessly apart. "What's the matter?" Barry asked, several times in fact, as blobs of light slipped across the bus window glass. "Is it something I did?" She shook her head, but couldn't bring herself to speak. She was angry at herself for feeling this way. Barry touched her arm, her chin, her hair, convinced that it was something he'd said, or done, and when he wasn't asking her to tell him, he sat quietly, eyeing the other passengers, racking his brains. The bus lurched around corners. When at last they got off, he blurted,

"All right, I'm sorry!"

Rita told him in a whisper not to be. But she didn't explain until later when she slipped naked into bed with him, and locked a leg over his, and reached across his chest and gripped his far shoulder. Her cheek lay on his breast, and she thought of Miüsov's love story, and of the aristocrat who died under sharpened birch sticks: nothing like that had truly happened to her. So as for tonight, what had she to fear? How could a movie condemn her soul? How could a little celluloid and light, artifice at every turn, exert real power? Surely another person's imagination reached only so far. Until recently she hadn't bothered about such thoughts; she couldn't muster belief. And now she still couldn't—yet somehow, she felt the pain.

"Listen," she said, "it's not you, BeeBee. Really. I just got to settle down. That movie upset me, that's all. I let it get to me. Why do I do that? Why should a person put herself through this? You don't let make-believe hurt you. It doesn't seem that way. You don't seek it out, do you?"

With a heaving of blankets he turned on his side, facing her. His hand moved between her breasts, down her belly. "What's to say?" Between her legs, then back up again, all the way to her forehead, where he pressed. "I mean, I know what's good for a person." He brought his mouth to her ear, brushing, then to the point of her chin. Then the tip of her breast. "Come here, you need me," he said. "Please."

A History of the Fruitcake

The first fruitcake was invented in 1723 by a syphilitic Bavarian baker named Karl Schneizenweizen, for which he was sentenced to twelve years in prison where he died before the end of his term, completely mad. But his invention lived after him and you can still see the original fruitcake in Schneizenweizen's hometown of Proeish (price of admission, two euros) where his creation is on display, mostly intact, for no one has been able to finish it. Legend has it that the famous first fruitcake has survived three fires, an earthquake and pestilence, famine, and most recently, the bombing of the town of Proeish by Allied forces in the Second World War in which all the buildings in the entire quarter were destroyed, *with the sole exception of the museum with the first fruitcake.*

Despite Schneizenweizen's ignominious death, his invention soon spread to other parts of Europe. The English in particular showed a genius for this perversion, quickly adapting their own versions, which gave rise to the creation of secret societies. Because of the tendency for fruitcake makers to attract abuse, in a short time the fruitcake arrived in America in the hands of devout, jowly dissenters fleeing persecution.

Today the United States is the largest producer of fruitcakes in the world, and the innovator of artificial coloring for its gooey composite fruit chunks. The United States is also the country with the largest number of fruitcake disposal sites (the life of a fruitcake being estimated by some scientists at 10,000 years), though new sites are being constructed by Halliburton KBR contractors in Honduras, Vietnam and Tanzania.

Some say the future of the fruitcake is in doubt. Many people wonder if it is safe, citing experiments in which fruitcakes have been demonstrated to cause nausea in laboratory mice. Yet sales remain steady, new investment in heavy production machinery is already under way, and many experts forecast a surge of fruitcakes in the 21st century.

This paper is printed on 100% recycled fruitcakes

AT THE LUXURY PET SHOPPE

Richard was impressed by the cat's pajamas. Such soft cotton! Were these microfibers or what?

And he lingered in wonder before the display of the dog's slinky negligée.

But for his precious little Tippy he would not, absolutely not, buy the parakeet's strapon dildo!

He slammed the door behind him.

WHY I WEAR A HAT

It's my horns. Let me explain. It seems so long ago though I recollect quite clearly the night I went to bed with a terrible headache. It had been an eventful day at work for the young up-and-coming fellow that I was then, dedicated to poise, excelling at interpersonal skills. In fact my co-worker Helen had told me that more than anyone in our department, I was the lubricant. This was a thrill! And what followed had nothing to do with—let me make this clear—my conduct.

I went to bed early that night, a grinding pain in my skull. Pulling off my clothes I wondered what could cause such pressure, such maddening prickling. Several times I tried to pound it back with my fist. Already I'd swallowed a handful of aspirins. In bed I swam in my sheets till at last sleep came to the rescue: I dreamed a comfortable mirror image of myself in bed, dreaming, with nothing strange happening that needed to be understood. (I was, if I may say so, a rather happy individual, extremely well-adjusted.) When I awoke early the next morning the pain was gone.

In fact I bounded out of bed like a champion. Then, while shaving, there was a surprise in the mirror.

Those bumps on my head! What were they? I touched them. Rubbed them. Bigger than bumps—little knobs, actually. The most curious thing. I tried to press the knobs back, but when I let off, they only looked pinker, and stood out more. In a fury I rubbed and rubbed—to no avail. The knobs tingled. In fact, they felt good.

That day I combed my hair down, managed to cover them, though I didn't like the idea of appearing so boyish when I was hoping for a promotion. A few colleagues gave me funny looks but I stared back so intently that they averted their eyes, moved away. *Go ahead*, I thought, *try to really see me!*

Wasn't long before Helen complimented my new style. Those were busy times at National Pharmaceutical, especially in the blood division where I worked. Once, after a whopping order of 3000 units, our sales ombudsman Charles Percival put down the phone and loosened his tie. His eyes shone with happiness. A smile crept onto his lips. Suddenly he leaped out of his chair, grabbed his umbrella and squeezed it like a cane:

> *"Start spreadin' the news*
> *My sales will astound..."*

Irrepressible Charlie, some called him. He loved our post-holiday rush, and dictated correspondence while doing his daily office workout (*"Go ahead, punch me in the stomach!"*). The only problem was (though I never said so to anyone, for interpersonal reasons) Charlie could be, well, tiresome. After work he asked me to accompany him to bars where he continued talking about price forecasts and insurance premium policy and other questions that haunted him.

I was more interested in Helen. When I could pull away from Charlie, I invited her to have dinner with me in some quiet, amber-lighted place with string music coming out of the plants. She was shy about herself at first, almost secretive, and very pale, but get a thick red steak in her and she would tell you her life's story, how she fought her way up the ladder at various Nat Pharm offices. I remember one special evening putting down a couple of Porterhouses after a hard day's work, the two of us sitting, making fists on the linen tablecloth, looking into each other's eyes. Me thinking: This is it. I've really found her.

Back then I wore my hair in a pompadour, which I let droop a little in front. She smiled back at me.

She first discovered my secret in bed. I'd forgotten myself, and she was running her hands through my hair.

"Hey. What are these?"

"What? Oh...nothing. I bumped my head. In the bathroom."

"On both sides?" She slid over, turned on the light. I lay blinking, not knowing what to say. "You've—you've got horns!" she said.

Already she was twisting away from me. Her face was agitated, her lips pressed together in horror.

"I won't hurt you," I whispered.

"But—but I've never been with a man with horns before." She repeated this several times, even lifting a hand before her face as if to hide behind it. Genuinely afraid, poor Helen. Although I couldn't justify myself, I tried to keep her close by, talking in a low, calm voice to let her hear *me*, to reassure her that it was only *me*, the same old *me*, the man she liked. She had nothing to be afraid of.

Eventually she relaxed, and conversed in a normal tone. She seemed convinced that there must be a logical explanation. "Is it hereditary? Are their antecedents? Do your parents have horns?" My answers were unsatisfactory. Not even aged photographs of great-grandparents and liverfaced aunts and skinny-rat uncles with yellow beards from the old country revealed (for of course I'd checked!) an ancestor with horns. Eventually Helen pushed a pillow on her lap, looked at me sideways, giggled. "Don't do that to your hair," she said.

I'd pressed it all the way down on my temples in my effort to appear less fearsome.

"Let me take another look."

Now it was my turn to be scared. My breaths came short as I reached up, swept my hair back. Would this ruin everything? She stared, even changed positions to see from another angle. After a pause, she asked to touch them. First she extended just a finger; moments later both thumbs pressed. Her puzzled expression didn't change, but her voice was unmistakably friendlier.

"Well, they are sort of cute."

Tears collected in the corners of my eyes. She saw this, and caressed my horns ever so gently. "It's all right, sweetie, it's all right." I embraced her, at this moment feeling more love than I'd ever felt for anyone. So intense was my embrace, my lips up and down her neck, then sliding shivery the other way, that the message definitely came through. She began nibbling at my horns. This virtually split me open with excitement. I answered her with passion, and soon the walls resounded with Helen's cries of delight.

In the weeks that followed we were almost never apart. We lived in a very pleasant confusion. "I never imagined I'd fall for a man like you," she told me one day as we lazied on a blanket on the floor, naked. She raised herself to one elbow and reached out, snapped her fingernail against a horn. *Tek.* "I...I never imagined a man like you."

"Me neither," I admitted.

She rolled over on her stomach.

"Run them down my back again. Don't stop till I tell you."

In those early days she liked to tease me by saying I reminded her of a fellow she'd read about in school, a guy who woke up one morning and discovered he was a big bug, or maybe it was a salamander, something like that. At any rate a very creepy dude.

I didn't think much of the comparison, and eventually blurted:

"Helen, that's not my story. You've got it turned around. A person like that couldn't go on functioning, hold a job, do something positive for society. Is that my case? I am, if I may say so, an asset to the community. A solid citizen! Not some weirdo. People *like* me."

Her eyes grew. "Oh, I'm sorry. Yes, yes, it's true—you do so well, you help everything along. Come here now."

She reached for my ears. "Sweetie, you're the lubricant." Humbly, I bowed my head, and she kissed my tips.

❋

Helen's family, however, was less appreciative. In fact her parents caused a rift that threatened to keep us apart forever. They let it be known that they strongly disapproved of my extra-cranial protrusions.

This stung. After all, other people had acted impressed, for I'd started showing my horns openly, sweeping my hair back at moments when I knew someone was watching. Oh, that careless toss, practiced in front of a mirror! Such was the response that maybe I'd become a bit vain. Accustomed to others' ahhing. So her parents' reaction came as a blow.

"I'm afraid I'll have to ask you to leave this house," announced Mr. Wilkinson softly, while an entire side of Mrs. Wilkinson's face trembled. "I won't pretend with you. We've never had horns in our family, and I don't see why we should start now."

Helen stared at the floor, her eyes pained. "Dad," she said, "Dad—"

"I'm sorry, but that's the way your mother and I feel. Right, Lucy?"

"Yes, Edgar." Then Mrs. Wilkinson rushed out of the room, pressing a tissue to her face.

Afterward, in the car, I thought Helen was going to apologize for her family. But she made a shocking admission. "Well, I *do* have doubts. Not about our affection for each other but about the way people will always misunderstand. We have to live with the rest of the world, too, we can't pretend it's not there. And we have to be brave enough to think about the long term. Can we really live with only us? Do we have a long term? Honestly, I don't know."

So it had come to this. Stricken, I lurched the car to the side of the road. The engine roared when I took it out of gear, then swung my door open. Helen called to me, "Wait! Where are you going?" as I staggered off into the night, clutching my horns.

The first couple of weeks of our separation were grueling. In my desperation to fill the void, I went on a binge with irrepressible Charlie. This part of my story is embarrassing to recount, but since I've committed myself to tell the truth, I confess that we made asses of ourselves: boogying in every bar on a 3-mile strip, Charlie flashing his money, his bald head pulsing under disco strobe lights, laughing, crowing, teeth reflecting, slipping his arms around teetering females who watched in amazement as I impaled cans of beer on my horns and directed geysers of yellow foam down my throat. Everyone cheered!

Well, you had to be there. Still it was surprising, the stir we caused, Charlie waving his money and buying everyone rounds while still gibbering about record sales while my eyes searched through the bodies and smoke and fixed on a wavy-haired woman with flag lipstick—oh, that mouth!—it was impossible not to stare, and she stared back, her front teeth biting her stars and stripes, inspiring me with a throb of patriotism such as I'd never felt before. She accompanied me to the toilet where I put in the first quarter, she the second, she put her hand on mine and we turned the knob together, holding each other up, rocking unsteadily on our feet, waiting for the condom to fall: she sighed, and God, it was romantic...

Then it got strange. The people we met. Gwendolyn and her fun cage! After a couple of weeks non-stop, I had to quit. Charlie, who declared that a good roll in the gutter was purifying, wasn't about to let up, and reported to his desk every morning and rolled up his sleeves for another day's work. *How* did he do it? I, in contrast, stumbled in with my jaw sagging, a cold sweat on my forehead, veiny pouches under my eyes. Each time I blinked, there was a scraping like crushed glass. Once I dashed out to the plaza in front of our building and barfed on the company tulips.

Then an official letter arrived on my desk, bearing the signature and seal of the Nat Pharm CEO. I was hereby notified of a forced leave of absence, three weeks, unpaid, followed by a year's probation.

This shook me. It was a wake-up call. Surely I'd have to pull myself together and try something else. Life must be more than a search for sensation—gusto to the max—horny deliria. From overuse, my extremities were growing numb. What I needed was something beyond myself. *Someone.* And who this person was, I already knew.

Helen. How could I win her back?

My chance finally came one afternoon while Charlie was out of the office defending my job to the department head, and suddenly Helen appeared before me, gazing with a pitying tenderness. I got down on my knees, tried to remind her of the old days, of what we had lost and what would could share again.

"I don't know," she replied, tearful, "I just don't know." She gripped my horns while I vowed that I would always be there, she could steer me according to her needs.

"Please say yes."

"Oh, it's so confusing, baby."

"You can count on me to be everything humanly possible!"

"That I *do* know."

She backed up and I followed on my knees till she came to rest on the edge of my desk and sat on a productivity profile. Winning Helen over took a stupendous amount of wooing, a tireless tongue. And a solemn promise that whenever I was in the presence of her parents, or people like them, I would respect a certain decorum. I would wear a hat.

Strange to think that this now integral part of my appearance, which I've grown to relish, started amidst crisis. But no matter. On my wedding day I wore a tall black top hat (cutting a strikingly Lincolnesque figure, if I may say so) discovering, to the wonderment and admiration of guests who also wore hats that afternoon but had the damnedest time keeping them on (it was a blustery Saturday)—horns were practical! Kept my stovepipe firmly in place. And later, after I became a father and Little League coach, it was an effective technique indeed to pause a moment in the late innings and take off my cap, wipe my brow, tell the team that it was time to pull together, to rally, to (here I touched the tip of each horn for emphasis) GO GET 'EM! And my, how they whooped in response! I was a *very* successful Little League coach.

But I'm getting ahead of myself. My quest to make sense and come to terms with my hornhood had, in reality, only begun. Helen and I agreed that we wanted to settle down, start a family, and after our honeymoon in Vera Cruz (Qué fiesta! the beaches! my sombrero!), we knew it was time to devote our lives to something other than work. Another force was shaping our future. Irrepressible Charlie was sorry to see us go, actually peeved ("Leave now? When we got demand comin' out the yinyang?") but we'd made up our minds, and applied for transfers to the records department. Here, though the money was less attractive and there was none of the pulsing excitement of our previous jobs, we could live for something besides the company. We did it, I like to think, out of a larger sense of humanity.

Our baby boy looked just like me! I confess that from his infancy onward I often passed my hand across his head on the pretext of a caress, or, playfully, to muss his hair, searching for little bumps. But I found none. And throughout Marvin's adolescence, despite occasional thwarted hopes (just pimples), no new horny extrusions came into my life.

But why did it matter if Marvin had horns? Why did I wish intensely that little pointed tips nestled in his Boy Scout cap, just as manly barbs rose beneath my drill hat, as leader of Troop 167? Why, when Melissa was born two years later, a tiny dynamo of energy throughout her girlhood, did I fantasize two budding horns in perfect symmetry with her pigtails? Why this overwhelming, egotistical desire for a continuation—a confirmation—of myself?

If I was insecure, if the mirror sometimes inspired fear and pity, it was because I was desperate to understand what they *meant*, atop my head, the only globe whose existence I was sure of, the only world I knew! Why were there horns on it? Why? The passing of time had changed nothing. Here, I discovered, was my true quest in life: why I wear a hat.

At first it was tempting to blame someone else. For instance I asked myself: could Helen be untrue to me?

Now, certainty was impossible on such a question. And I'm not a superstitious man. But I'd seen an old movie on TV about an English tavern owner whose wife cheated on him behind the bar and as a result, he grew horns. It was some kind of folk magic, supposed to be funny. Sometimes, rubbing my own horns, I felt a flippy, nervous doubt. Could Helen do that to me?

Over the years she'd remained an attractive woman, zesty, with a soft plum mouth and marked appetites. It required no great effort to imagine her enjoying admirers. I'm not jealous by nature but sometimes I wondered...

Yet Helen would've denied this possibility, and what's more, gave me no reason not to believe her. Chronology was on her side, too: my horns had appeared *before* our relationship really got under way. So a link with infidelity, real or imagined, didn't wash.

Moreover Helen has always found me, if I may say so, rather deeply satisfying. To this day she delights in donning her translucent red silk cape, teasing in circles around the bedroom. "Olé! Señora Toréador!"

Or: could these curious protuberances which surely have roots near my brain suggest something—one hates to use the obvious words—*devilish? Evil?*

Now, I don't pretend to be perfect. In my life I've done things that I'm ashamed of, and have already mentioned some of them. If my sins aren't as numerous as the grains of sand on a beach, they are, let's say, like the number of leaves in a forest. In full summer.

On the other hand, though I realize that being a substitute deacon at Garden City United Methodist Church will not earn me a special place in heaven, that struggling to avoid using swear words in front of the children does not equal heroism, that throwing away the orgy butter saved from my nights in Gwendolyn's fun cage (would it someday come in handy again?) is not the true meaning of sacrifice, I *have* suffered for my crown of horns. And have acted no more the devil than my peers.

Consider: For years I ran 15 miles every Memorial Day to raise money for the kids at Camp Koestler, and volunteered summers as a counsellor. Photographs downstairs of me and the kids in wheelchairs, kids I love, all of us wearing 10 gallon buckaroo Texans for the Wild West Show we put on for Parents' Weekend. I mention this not to brag, I promise not to parade out all my plaques, but this is just one example out of many. I've proved myself time and time again! What about those long hours spent as an organizer of the New Year's Eve Ball at St. Agathe's Burn Ward? Oh, the moment when the band struck up Auld Lyne Syne and I took Helen in my arms, a cone with foiled streamers on my head, my eyes beginning to leak. "*Why?*" I wondered, "*why?*"

I consulted many doctors. (Was I a hiccup of Nature, an innocent victim of biological sabotage?) Even managed to wangle an appointment with Li Seng, the Nobel Prize winning veterinarian, when he was at nearby Barkley College on a lecture tour. He affixed electrodes, measured with calipers, took X-rays and made a hot wax impression of the top half of my skull. He monitored blood flow with an ultrasonic spectrum analyser, via a cool acoustic gel applied to some of the most sensitive parts of my person. Then he informed me through a translator that everything about me was most ordinary.

Was this what I wanted to hear? Would others believe it? I bid goodbye to Doctor Li who blinked at me through his glasses as I left the consultation room and his instruments. Exiting the building, I went to the parking lot and climbed into my car and sat behind the wheel with the windows rolled up. For more than a minute, I didn't start the engine. Rocking in my seat, slapping the steering wheel and pounding my feet on the floor, I howled.

My social circle was no help. In the course of my quest, despite my habitual discretion, it was impossible to keep my barbs a complete secret. Family, friends and most of my colleagues were aware of what I kept under my hat. Somehow word even got round to a newspaper of scurrilous reputation, found in supermarkets everywhere. One morning, upon opening the door to let out the cat, I was startled by a *snick snick snick* from the flower-bed: a camera was pointed at me like a black-snouted automatic weapon.

"Asshole!" I shouted. "What the hell do you think you're doing?"

The asshole scampered through begonias.

By sheer luck, I'd been wearing the knit nightcap the kids had got me for Christmas, so I wasn't too troubled about exposure. But later the same day the phone rang and it was an editor from the East Coast. After I refused each of his arguments and sizeable cash offers, he threatened to run a doctored picture of his own devising.

Now this was a fix. Why couldn't they leave a regular guy and good citizen alone? They had no right to cheapen my reputation! That night, as I grimly stood in front of the TV, my hand on the console and tilting my head to the left (in those days, it was the only way to get rid of the snowy picture), Helen came up with an ingenious excuse: "Why don't you just call that sleaze and tell him the whole thing's a hoax? That's why you won't cooperate. Act contrite. Tell him that in reality, you have no horns."

Simple—but therein was the beauty! I grabbed the phone, and fabricated a confession. Pretended to be sorry. I was a lonely person, he heard me say, hungry to be liked. My need was so strong. My horns, alas, were implants.

To my amazement, he replied, "That's all right, Mister. Just a twenty minute photo session and you'll get your two thousand bucks. But that means you sign the exclusive rights for us."

I slammed down the receiver. Oh, the insult! How clear it was now, his indifference to the true plight of horndom. This cut deeper than any shabby publicity. With grim determination I resolved not to cooperate with others' beliefs about me, and if necessary, to fight. During this period I never ventured out of the house without headgear that included a chin-strap, such as my orange metalflake motorcycle helmet—just try to pull it off me, you bastards!—or a leather WWII pilot's cap that had belonged to my father-in-law Edgar. I started carrying a shoulderslung pistol, too.

In time the paparazzi backed down, eventually settling for a similar story of a horned man in Stockton, California—the grainy photo surely a fake—who no doubt accepted a lower price.

As for the rest of the world, the non-initiates, when in succeeding decades they saw me and my hat as inseparable, at parties, baptisms and once, a television game show, they might suspect that I was trying to play the dandy, or like others of the select few who still favor fedoras, I was bald. They believed they were humoring me. But in fact, they were the dupes.

Inevitably such trials affected my inner life. I grew increasingly philosophical under my beret. Sometimes speculating: *The reason must be bigger than me.* There was a tiny, persistent voice that seemed inspired of another source: *What if God intended my horns as part of the cosmic design?*

Perhaps it was inevitable that my horns should take me further afield. After all these years of searching it became easy to feel that I'd been singled out. Me: a truly unique case. And then, as if in answer to my premonition, I began hearing stories of a Nebraskan holy man, a person of remarkable powers, an irreproachable individual who transformed people's lives. He revealed their purpose.

All other paths had failed me. At this point, the idea that there was a Wise Person who might know was positively tantalizing.

I took a leave of absence from work, caught a flight to a sun-baked central city where I rented a bullet-shaped foreign car and traveled hard all day, barrelling down interstate arteries, burning up two-lane black-tops. Criss-crossing hay fields and soy bean capitals, eventually navigating through the blinding dust of gravel roads on the directions of natives using only silos for landmarks. Into the deepest heartland.

At the end of my road, a neat white farmstead shimmered in the afternoon sun. With friendly, peppery barks, a collie ran forward to greet me.

In the front yard men and women of various ages were throwing and chasing frisbees. Green, blue, yellow frisbees spun through the air. Girls in tank-tops, guys in skate-board gear, and—over there—was that Dick Cheney in shorts? I stepped uncertainly out of my car, let the collie sniff me, and then asked a tall blond fellow who loped by where I could find his leader. He swung his arm. "Up there, on the porch."

So I crossed the yard, dodging the players and passing a rhubarb patch on my way up the front steps of the house where I found a wiry, handsomish man in his fifties with a brown, weather-beaten face. Sitting beside him on the porch swing was a grey-haired woman of about the same age, with glasses, slightly plump. They were conversing softly, swinging, and fell silent when I drew near.

"What can I do for you?" he asked.

The woman looked me up and down. For a moment the only sounds were shouts from the front yard, and the steady creak of chains of their swing. I was unsure how to begin.

"Stranger, you can tell me," the man encouraged. "We're all friends here."

So, awkwardly, in bits and swallowed rushes, I told him about my problem. Why I wore a hat. Both listened without interruption, and when I finished, the man said,

"That's a new one on me. Let me see 'em."

He sounded sympathetic. The woman shifted and leaned forward, interested. I fingered the brim of my slouch porkpie. When I took it off, I could tell they were impressed. Their eyes bore in on me. "Can I touch 'em?" he asked.

I nodded, bowing closer, whereupon he seized my horns roughly. For a few panicky seconds I thought he was trying to hurt me, maybe wanted to take me down and bind my hands and ankles, so I resisted with all my strength. We twisted across the length of the porch, and just when I thought I might get the upper hand, he used a technique which to this day I don't understand. Next thing, there was a crash—*me*—and I looked up at him dazedly from the floorboards.

"Hmmm," he said, rubbing his palms. "Sorry about that. But I had to make sure they were real."

"We get all kinds," the woman said.

I sat up, ruefully straightening the hair around my horns.

"I'll see what I can do," he said, and the screen door clapped behind him.

As I dusted myself off, rubbing a sore elbow, she smiled at me, inquired if she could feel my horns, too. Cautiously I bent toward her, bracing myself. But she was gentle, and remained seated on the swing. "Isn't that something?" she remarked, laughing in a high voice, plucking at first one, then the other. "They seem to suit you, too, I mean they're not upsetting to look at, not like the two-headed calf at the fair." As she squeezed my horns, her voice was soothing and friendly, and I looked down the front of her dress, at her big round breasts. The screen door banged and her husband came out brandishing a sickle—or so I thought at first as I straightened up fast and moved away, slapping on my hat.

"This used to belong to the kids," he said, pensively. "You know how to work a boomerang?"

I shook my head. "No."

"Don't hurry off. Just listen. Dot will show you how to throw it, she's better at it than I am. Dot?"

The woman stepped down from the porch swing and we followed her into the front yard. The frisbees stopped flying as the players respectfully paused to watch. Dot stood beside me, explained how to hold the boomerang. "We mail-ordered it," she said, rehearsing a back-handed motion. "It's pretty simple, really. You'll get the hang."

Dot reared, then unleashed. The boomerang spun out of the yard, over nearby trees and electric wires into the sky where it seemed to hang for a moment, like a bird changing its mind, and then suddenly it dropped out of the blue and swooped past the electric wires into the yard where I stood transfixed as it hummed with increasing velocity toward the top of my head. At the last second a hand clamped down on my shoulder, saved me. I hit the ground hard, and the boomerang crashed into the porch latticing behind us.

Dot sat up beside me. "Catching is trickier," she said.

Her husband was silent at first. He went over and picked the boomerang out of the marigolds. "It's all right," he called to the line of frisbee players. "You can go on." They turned away, filtering out over the grass, and resumed throwing. Now he said to us, tight-lipped:

"Dang, Dot. You're showin' off."

His voice was so soft as to be almost inaudible, but its effect on her was immediate. Dot's eyes glistened. Her nostrils reddened, and twitched. She ventured no reply. He handed me the boomerang.

They followed me to the car with the collie at their heels and, just before we said goodbye, I looked jealously at the people tossing frisbees. Why couldn't I do that instead?

He shook his head. "You just do the best you can," he told me.

"What do *you* do?" I demanded. "What do *you* throw?"

"Nothing." Then he smiled, reached into his back pocket. "Almost forgot. You try this on." He straightened a seed-cap, adjusted the plastic tabs in back, and handed it to me. I removed my hat and accepted his gift, put it on. (How did he know my size?) As I drove away he and Dot waved at me in my mirror.

❋

For weeks I kept the boomerang buried away in a drawer with my underwear and manly musky soaps. Telling myself I'd forget about it. You should remember that I was no longer a young buck. Grey hairs sprouted around my points. Despite my efforts to buff and brush, using fluoride preparations and hydrogen peroxide and commercial Pearl Drops, the day came when I had to admit the obvious: my horns were yellowing. Youth had abandoned me. Both my children were dating, Helen had acquired creases in the corners of her mouth and we'd fallen into a life of remote control, diet cream sodas and frequent flying. What was a man like me to do with this— this *toy?*

Yet I'd attempted everything else...till one sunny day I broke down and went to the bedroom chest of drawers and dug out the boomerang. I held it up to the window-light. All right, I thought. This is it. Make or break. If you couldn't trust Dot, who could you trust?

I went to the park. And soon discovered that throwing a boomerang is no easy stunt. I've always been rather athletic, if I may say so, Helen has described me as graceful, a quality I've maintained even as my shorts

111

grow tighter. But this ridiculous trifle, I couldn't get it to work.

When I threw, it refused to come back. Every time! I tried and tried, but the boomerang never changed direction, spinning off with no return, and then there was a long, lonely run to where it had landed in the grass. I would heave again—off it sailed, away, away! I chased that damn boomerang all over the park. It was exhausting.

Yet I continued, for there was always hope that if my technique were adjusted this way or that, the boomerang would respond. I imitated Dot as closely as possible, and when that failed, I began experimenting. Arcing at various angles, or tossing with a distinct upward slice.

Always, however, it went *away*.

"Son of a bitch!" I exclaimed, huffing across the green, holding my side. "Why won't it work? Why?" Joggers turned their heads, and I pushed past shuffling oldsters and couples with baby strollers. On my way to a flower bed. I ripped my boomerang out of the azaleas.

Panting, I coiled, and then unleashed with all my might, shouting like an Olympian, "*Aaaaaah!*"

Off it soared over the duck pond.

My stomach began to churn. Blood beat in my ears. "No!" Yet I began the long run around the water, and eventually spied my boomerang stuck in a hedge. I staggered toward it.

Just what was the point here? I wondered, sweat stinging my eyes and a taste on the back of my tongue like a dissolving penny. What? You could throw, and throw, and throw. On and on, following till you went round the world! And then where would you be? I seized the boomerang out of the leaves. Trying to laugh but finding it almost impossible for lack of air. *Right where you started!*

Gasping, I stumbled on, weaving under the trees with their sticky leaves. My chest convulsed. Oh, give me air!

And what, I asked myself as the horizon wheeled and blurred before my eyes, what if I mastered this fucking boomerang, and could throw it perfectly? So it came back every time, right on the money? Where would I be?

With a little scream I cried out, *"Right where I started!"*

I slid down to the ground, helplessly twitching and momentarily deprived of my faculties. Whispering to the boomerang, gurgling, using one end to scratch between my horns. "Ooohhh. Ooohhh."

Hard to say how long this state lasted. Eventually, though, I remembered I was in a public place and pulled myself to my feet, hastily wiped the spittle from my face, beat the dust off my pants. Ran a hand over my head, to fix my hair around my...hell, I thought, where's my straw Panama?

Lost.

In my dismay I noticed a man on a bench nearby, feeding popcorn to pigeons. With embarrassment, I wondered if I should explain myself. But then it became obvious there was something terribly wrong with him.

Pigeons perched on the bench, the man's knees, his shoulders. His trembling hand reached into a crumpled paper bag, and when the hand reappeared, clutching popcorn, a great fluttering arose. The pigeons didn't wait for him to throw the popcorn but attacked the hand, in seconds covering it with welts.

Yet the hand did not jerk away. Slowly it returned to the bag. I looked at the man's face, the dome of his head spotted with welts, too. Shining beads of blood. In shock I realized: yes, I knew this man!

A swirl of pigeons rose, his face disappeared. They tore the bag away from him. Then he reappeared, his head teetering in a palsy.

"Charlie? Is that you?" I cried.

Slowly he lifted his eyes.

"Charlie—that *is* you!"

"Oh. Hello. Who are you?"

"Don't you remember me? My God!" I came to him, waving my arms and kicking at pigeons. "Shoo! Shoo!" The birds gurred; feathers flew. "Oh Charlie, Charlie, this is terrible. I didn't even recognize you. My God, what's happened to you?"

His eyes moved deep in their sockets.

"I'm—I'm repressed now."

Speechless, I gripped my boomerang, and he bowed his head.

I fell onto the bench beside him and he slumped forward even further, chewing his lips. It was ghastly. The thing to do, I told myself, was to throw an arm around him, offer some consolation. Be a friend. But his bloody welts, the forced, raspy sound of his breathing and especially, the runny birdshit on his clothes, repulsed me. My voice came out shaky:

"I'm sorry, old man, I really am. You know I'm truly sorry. I just can't—"

At this point I broke off completely, looking up at the trees, trying to get a fix. *How? Dear Lord.* Then, forcing myself, gathering up all the concentration I could muster, I slung my arm around him, his filthy rags and bones, and we rocked for several minutes, not saying a word. Eventually my composure returned, and I started talking about the old days. "We sure had some fun, didn't we now? And laughs? Boy, old pard, when I think back, those days down on the Pharm... Remember Gwendolyn? Holy—"

"Why did you scare them away?"

"Huh?"

"Whadya go and do that for?"

His grimace, exposing his teeth, gave him an expression remarkably skull-like. When I left Charlie, told him good-bye, he didn't answer. I don't think he was trying to be rude. He stared off into space. His future was as plain as the blood on his face.

The boomerang hangs in the den above my trophy shelf, among plaques and photographs and certificates of award, beside my gold-embroidered fez as Grandmaster of the Loyal Order of Moose Lodge 206. The kids' graduation pictures are up there too, and Melissa's army portrait, as well as Helen's snapshot of her parents, Edgar and Lucy, gaping on their 50th wedding anniversary. Oh well. I guess it's everybody's wall now.

In the basement is a room where sometimes I go to use my horns. Actually, *using* them is the closest thing to relief. Over the years, I've tried many targets, but have to admit that this wall is as good as anything I've found.

I butt it. *Bang.* It's more than a pastime. *Bang.* No special equipment is required. No fancy shoes. Once you start, it's hard to stop. *Bang!*

Feels so real. Look for an unblemished spot on the wall. A run, a leap: *bang!*

Once I got stuck up there for twenty goddamn minutes, yelling intermittently, till Helen and the kids pulled me down. While waiting I had plenty of time to think. And curse. Yet the first thing I did when free was to give another buck.

My straight-on freight train smash! *Bang!* Tears come. Sing hosanna to all creation, here is my personal rhythm contribution: *Bang! Bang!*

A stunner. But when I open my eyes again—like a miracle each time, as long as it will last—I pull myself to my feet. Straighten my clothes. Climb the stairs, toward everything. And before I go outside, I put on my hat.

THE LEO INTERVIEW

"Regrets are too easy. Remorse spun pure—that would be more like it."

So says Leo, though in a tone that is anything but severe. In fact, his most striking feature, even more than a still imposing physical presence, is his chipper spirit. Like a breeze it wafts through the uptown sunbeams entering his apartment at the Althea where walls are studded with photographs of a career spanning generations. Above the exercise bike with four pedals, faces and accolades of those as iconic as himself, interspersed with publicity stills of the once famous, now forgotten, and the smiles of unknowns. All paying tribute.

"Remorse about what?"

"Oh, not remorse of the ordinary sort. You know." He laughs. "That's hardly me."

Chipper, yes, but Leo has never been one for modesty. Informality makes no difference, and in fact allows him to press his advantage. He conducted this interview wearing only a lemon chiffon robe. The famous mane is thinner now, grayer, and a conspicuous paunch swells where the satin sash is loosely tied, an immodesty which only the force of his personality saves—just barely—from an appearance of being crude. His tail, which in conversation he will seize and shake at you to underline a point, is combed to a glossy tossle at the end. Finely powdered, too, with a scent of gardenia, if this interviewer's nostrils may be trusted. Despite his years he remains undeniably handsome.

"In the beginning we were all just so busy, we didn't have time, my friend, to think about remorse or anything along those lines. Wasn't till later, maybe the first USO tour, that what I was doing began to be more than just work and assume a sort of weight." (As he says this, one's eyes inevitably stray to the framed photograph on the nearby grand piano, of a helmeted Leo in a jeep with Eisenhower.) "I was going through a bad marriage at the time. All the travel and the rest of it. Europe was a mess, you can't imagine the conditions we had to put up with for the show! We had a bunch of skinny little guys, Alsatians I think, running in a circle around a big wheel under the stage just so we could get enough electricity for the lights. Where was I? Oh, yeah: telegrams about the divorce, and me doing the same song and dance every night. The roar, of course. I couldn't wait to leave. Then I realized there was no home waiting for me to go back to."

More than half a century ago—when Leo started making the entire world his home. In the process he made his share of enemies, too, participated in some colossal flops, even embarrassed himself. Yet all but the most sour of his critics acknowledge the extent to which he appealed to millions. And they all agree on the reason why: The Roar.

Audiences in theaters the world over thrilled to his signature cry. It was a call to dreams, a preamble to romance as couples clutched each other in the dark. Children tingled with awe and anticipation of adventure. Leo brought it all. *The promise!* Leo felt like everything America might hope it could be; in a precious way, Leo *was* America. After such a performance, how could he ever top himself?

So much has been said, with hyperbole the common currency, that it is difficult to keep a sense of perspective. One must nonetheless ask: why this Leo? Many a show business lion, arguably as sleek, young, and charming, had preceded him. Why did not some other handsome cat break through the circus circuit before him? Clocking 5.87 seconds, how did his roar become The Roar?

Though many have pointed to its potent mix of power and desire, what is often overlooked is its spontaneity. If for just a moment one can ignore that astounding baritone, bared teeth: how disarmingly casual the young cat appears! Looks as if he's hardly trying. In fact, for all the bravado, Leo's is a performance of remarkable restraint. Behind the searing youthful magnetism, there is a preternatural maturity. The result: genius.

"It took us twenty-three takes," he admits surprisingly. "Back then, to tell the truth, I didn't know what I was doing. I was just young and hungry, that's all. They kept asking, so I kept trying. Back then, I had the chops. People don't realize how hard we worked in those days."

"Do you think it's different now?"

"Of course it's different now! You got talented performers but there's nothing to let people dream. That was the flip side to the hard work. Mount Olympus. We had the glamour, kiddo."

"Isn't it possible that audiences have changed? And was it really as glamorous as you say?"

Leo yawns an impressive yawn, almost like a roar with the sound turned off, while reaching into the front of his robe and idly scratching his belly. Uninterested in such discussions. "Then why are you sitting here talking to me?" he asks.

"Is it true DiMaggio came after you with a baseball bat?"

He stops scratching, half a grin appearing on his lower lip.

"Yeah. He caught us *in flagrante*. But let's get this straight: Marilyn would've never left him for me. There was nothing, like, *serious*. I almost got killed that night— no exit but through the window, and there wasn't even time to open it!" A shudder ripples through the folds of skin around his chin. "I don't blame him though. And Marilyn was a sweet kid, really sweet. It's too bad what happened to her later," he opines.

"You never lacked company, though. How do you account for the number of young women in your life? Is it just fame?"

"Oh, that's a lot of it, surely. But these wonderful ladies also need something, and I like to think that I've been there for them." He pauses, mouth pursed, eyes half-closed—somehow, for a reason Leo does not disclose but whose existence he nevertheless insinuates, his well-known predilection for starlets is necessary, even poignant. He leans closer, now nods. "Something else too. You might as well know. *It's the mane.* I mean, don't ask me why, but they just can't keep their hands off it, baby!"

Then he tosses his head back and laughs, laughs, and suddenly black ties fall loose above dinner jackets, cars sprout fins, the pack is back, and one is in the presence of an unreconstructed swinger—it's amazing, almost like meeting a Confederate general—a sensation that a moment later totally evaporates with a scuffling and tromp in the hallway. It's the arrival of Max, a bubbling three-year-old, who scampers into the room.

124

"Come here, dude! Come right here!" he cries, scooping up the young one as he trots by, adding, "It's all right, no problem," to the pierced nanny hovering at the threshold. "How was the park?" Leo booms.

"We saw the baby goats."

"You saw the baby goats!" Leo says to Max. "And how were the baby goats? How many did you see? What colors were they?"

Max looks around—a resemblance with his father is striking—but he doesn't have the answers, yet. He basks in the attention.

"You know, there's nothing like being a father again to get your feet back on the ground, to remind you of what really matters in life. What really matters to me is our trip to our place in the mountains this weekend. We're going to the mountains, aren't we, Maxie?"

Leo does appear calmer, even younger, with Max, and is avowedly grateful for what he describes as a second chance. (Vanessa, 44 years his junior, is for the record his fourth wife; she declined to participate in this interview.) Leo's earlier offspring grew up in the shadow of his career, and he speaks with open declarations of contrition about his failures as a father. Son Daryl died over 20 years ago, after a short stint fronting a rock band and series of small film roles; daughter Julie (the only one whose picture appears among the crowd of faces in this room) now lives quietly on the West Coast ("She's had her share of troubles, too. She opened a chain of health spas. We talk often on the phone"); the youngest, Geoffrey, remains estranged from his father, and in certain circles has acquired a notoriety of his own. Always the most political of Leo's brood, he denounced his father in the harshest of terms for the way he'd constructed his public image, feeding the crudest stereotypes of the King of the Jungle. Geoffrey left the U.S. and for years lived on the savannah, far from the world of his upbringing, and nowadays works as a grassroots activist.

"Oh, he has his reasons, I guess," Leo says now, though past retorts via the media were less conciliatory. "I just think he might see differently if we spent some time together, talked things out. That fuss about my spread in *National Geographic*—really I still don't see what the big deal was."

"Have you ever run down an oryx?"

"Brother, I don't know an oryx from a penguin! So I posed for a few shots. I *never* pretended I wasn't born in the Bronx. And let me add that being a zoo cub was no picnic—Geoff had it much, much softer, more than he'll ever know or admit, no matter how much he preaches. I meant no disrespect to anybody in Africa or to cats back home. Or to oryxes everywhere, for God's sake. It was just business. If you want to talk politics you're only going to put everyone to sleep."

"But there was a time when you did your share of talking politics."

"Not really. Or just a little. Probably was drunk when I said it."

"Was that the case for your remarks about Mao?"

"Huh? You got to be kidding. What was that?"

"This surfaced in a recent book by Frances Wilcox, professor of French and Film Studies at Duke University, a 1969 article on you in *Cahiers du cinéma* in which you said, according to her translation, 'Mao not only makes sense of the past, he is the future, too. My life had no meaning till I discovered Mao and the people's revolution.' And a bit further on: 'Purgative violence is necessary to construct the new revolutionary man.'"

"I said no such thing!"

"These statements are fabricated?"

"Sure they are! Come on, what do you think? Where have you been? And if they're not fabricated I was just fooling around, taking the air out. Those journalists print what they need you to say. Especially over there, nobody spoke enough of the same language that we even bothered to try. These serious little guys wrote their serious little articles, while Orson and I hung out at the rue de Buci. He was there at the same time, you know, sort of in exile, too, if you can call it that. He'd promised me the lead in *Lear*, he was going to play all three sisters, and we were waiting for the money so we could begin shooting, and in the meantime we went to our favorite rôtisserie where we had chicken-eating contests. We would say how much more subtle and sophisticated life was over there, how artists like us were better appreciated, and the journalists agreed, and quoted us on politics. One day, I swear, we ate 43 chickens. Yet the whole time we were plotting our return to the States. Orson wanted to drop the film and had it in his head that we should go back to America together, a triumphant return, I could be in his magic act. But I would have nothing of it."

Leo breaks off here, perhaps preferring to pass over what actually happened, the less-than-inspiring homecoming for a short-lived and quickly forgotten TV sitcom ("Pa's Paws"), several unfortunate record albums, guest cameos on reality shows and an act in Las Vegas (audiences of winter vacationers off charter planes really went to see The Sex Kittens, his high-stepping backup chorus, who appeared in see-through shorts), till he infamously hit bottom one night on a talk show when he took a swipe at the host, *griffes sorties*, after a remark that he construed as insulting to his dignity. Tabloid photos of the time show a bloated, bedraggled Leo with a snarl on his lip as he ascends the courthouse steps.

Then the stay at the Betty Ford clinic. More than a few observers assumed that Leo was washed up. With intervening years, some even presumed him dead. In a bizarre footnote to his life story, a mentally ill airline pilot named Dexter Wills started claiming to be Leo, gave interviews and signed autographs and even managed to get hired as a PR spokesman for the Department of Homeland Security until, when doubts about his true identity surfaced, he called a press conference and tragically turned a gun on himself. That was more almost a decade ago but the story still fuels Internet conspiracies.

Yet since such low points, Leo's rehabilitation has been astonishing. And he has accomplished it, one must conclude, not through new projects or career gambles— Leo is now notoriously chary of his time, selective of public appearances, and interviews such as this one virtually unheard of—but through stubborn survival. Indifferent to this year's or next year's fashion.

"Is it true you turned down *Cats*?"

Leo sighs, shrugs.

"Well, I could never get on board. We were approached, yes, but negotiations went nowhere. The title was a sticking point. Why the plural?"

"What's next?"

Leo sniffs the air. "Who's to know? *Why know?* Bye, dude!" he calls to Max as he runs from the room, disappearing into the sun's glare from which a slim white hand emerges, and leads him away.

Since stage, screen and television are no longer Leo's chosen venues, and websites the ephemeral creations of fans and enthusiasts over which he has no control, perhaps this interview offers the role he wants to play today. The best way to burnish his image and define his niche in American culture. He is frank about this.

"Even though I know what's more important now, and my family comes first, I still like the fuss. I still hunger for something to show, sure."

"What would you consider appropriate?"

"Several congressmen are proposing a postage stamp. That would be OK, I guess."

"But you spoke of remorse. Let's come back to that. What remorse?"

"Well"—he searches. "It's like I haven't found a role as great as my promise. Yeah, that's it. So much has happened yet it doesn't add up to what at one time seemed possible. It wasn't just me who thought so, either. Everybody seemed to believe it. There was a time, a lost time—a beautiful time, truly—when I was part of something too big to fit on a postage stamp. Why should we settle for that?"

Leo gets up suddenly as if to put things right this instant. He advances to the window, looks back, beckons with a paw. Half a beat later his tail repeats the gesture with a lurid swish. (Was it on purpose, or some nervous shtick?) "Come here, kid, take a look."

The view of Central Park, the leaves of treetops shimmering, the spiny backbone of the island protruding nakedly and beyond, the deep, deep swirling orange of Everything West.

"What are you going to do with it," he asks, "after I'm gone and it's yours?"

Book Club Questions

Book Club Questions

1. Compare your chthonic desires to the ones in *Dick Cheney in Shorts*. Are they shared by other members in your group?

2. Would you rather have Herb's design for a pen (as described in "The Plans") or a real humdinger (see "Goodness Like a Fetter"). Explain your choice.

3. Do you think enhanced interrogation would improve the honesty of discussion in your group?

4. *"The mystery of life isn't that the world is so horrible. Or so beautiful. It's that it's so horrible and beautiful at the same time."* (Pyotr Miüsov) Discuss.

5. How would you answer Leo's question at the end of *Dick Cheney in Shorts*?

Charles Holdefer lives in Brussels. His novel *The Contractor*, about American use of torture in the "War on Terror," was chosen by the American Booksellers Association as a "Book Sense Pick" and has been translated into several languages. His short fiction has appeared in the *New England Review*, *North American Review*, *Chicago Quarterly Review* and elsewhere, and has been awarded a Pushcart Prize. He also writes essays, poetry and book reviews.

www.charlesholdefer.com